To Katie
Happy Christmas
Love
Mc

I.

First published in Great Britain in 1987 by
Methuen Children's Books Ltd,
11 New Fetter Lane, London EC4P 4EE.

Printed and bound by L.E.G.O., Vicenza,
Italy for Sadie Fields Productions Ltd,
London.

ISBN   0416   96760   4

The Night-Time Story

Karen Erickson and Maureen Roffey

Methuen

Everything is dark.
I can't see anything.

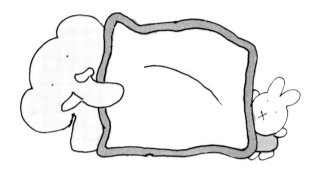

I wonder what's here,
or there,
or anywhere.

But wait.
I can be brave at night.

My room is the same.
Only the lights are out.

My window is fine.
Only the blinds are down.

My walls are the old daytime ones.

The floor is quiet.
Those shapes are my toys in the corner.

I know my room is safe.

Darkness makes everything
look different,
but it's the same.

Night is a soft blanket that comforts my room and lets it sleep.

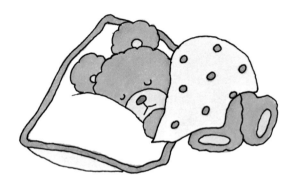

My room and I are sleepy.

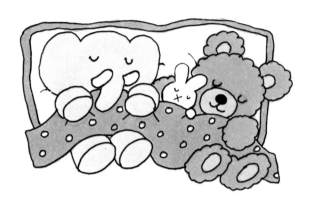

Look. I can be brave at night.
I can do it!